MonKey Me AND THE New Neighbor

BY
TIMoTHY RoLAND

BRANCHES

SCHOLASTIC INC.

Read all the **Monkey Me** books!

#1

#2

#3

#4

Table of Contents

To Beth, Matt, Andy, Stephanie, Janet,
Josh, Malachi, Kody, Kessiah, Darlene,
Jon, David, and Daniel.
-T.R.

Library of Congress Cataloging-in-Publication-Data Available

ISBN 978-0-545-55986-7 (hardcover) / ISBN 978-0-545-55984-3 (paperback)

10 9 8 7 6 5 4 3 2 1   14 15 16 17 18 19/0

Printed in China   38
First Scholastic printing, July 2014

Book design by Liz Herzog

chapter 1
Something Special

I looked in my desk drawers. And under my bed. And on my shelves.

"You should have looked for and found something yesterday, Clyde," Claudia, my twin sister, said. "Like I did."

I raced downstairs and into the kitchen.

"Sit and eat, Clyde!" Mom said.

"I can't. I need to find something special for today's show-and-tell." I grabbed a banana off the table and took a bite.

"Three weeks ago I brought my dinosaur model," I said. "And two weeks ago I brought my toy Golden Monkey."

"And last week," Claudia said, "you brought a banana." She chuckled.

"Don't remind me!" I said.

But my sister was right. Like usual.

I had forgotten to bring something to last week's show-and-tell. All I could find to show was the banana from my lunch bag.

I like bananas.

But everyone in my class laughed.

And laughed.

It had made me want to run and hide. That's why I needed to bring something super special this time.

I looked around the kitchen and saw some pink plastic flowers. A cup with a clown face on it. One cookie left in the cookie jar.

I reached toward it.

"Why don't you bring your pet monkey to show-and-tell, Clyde?" Mom said.

I stopped reaching.

Mom smiled. "A monkey is special."

"Yes. But . . ." I looked at Claudia. She didn't know what to say, either.

It started two weeks ago. My class was on a field trip to the science museum.

And Mom believed us.

At least, so far.

"And where is your pet monkey now, Clyde?" Mom asked.

"He should be outside," I said. Claudia followed as I ran toward the front door.

Then I stopped.

"Wait!" I said. "I know what I can bring for show-and-tell."

I raced upstairs and pulled a box of baseball cards from my bedroom closet. I grabbed my Clyde Spinner card.

He was a great baseball player. A pitcher. And he had a great first name — Clyde!

It was my favorite baseball card.

I dashed outside to where my sister was standing on our front lawn.

I couldn't wait to get to school. I couldn't wait for show-and-tell.

"Look, Clyde!" Claudia pointed across our lawn. "We're getting new neighbors!"

chapter 2
Uh-Oh! Roz!

Claudia and I ran to the front of the house next to ours. It had been empty for over two months.

But now we were getting new neighbors!

I saw a man carry a box out of a large truck. "Welcome to the neighborhood!" I shouted.

The man looked at me, confused.

Claudia chuckled.

"I'm just a mover, kid," the man said. "Your new neighbors won't be here until this afternoon."

I watched the man carry the box into the house. "I can't wait to see who's moving in," I said to Claudia.

"Neither can I," she said.

"Maybe it will be a family with a boy to play with," I said.

"Or a girl to play with," my sister said.

"Or a monkey to play with." I grinned.

Claudia rolled her eyes. "We'll find out after school."

"Then let's move!" I ran all the way to school and onto the playground. Claudia followed behind me.

Sometimes, running makes the day go faster. Sometimes, it gets me in trouble.

But it was okay for me to run on the playground. I just had to be careful not to run into anything.

Or anybody.

Like Principal Murphy!

I saw her on the other side of the playground. She looked angry. Like usual.

I turned to run the other way, and . . .

KA-BUMP!

Suddenly, I was on my back.

"Ha-ha! Squashed you!" Roz said.

I looked up at the class bully. She was standing on her skateboard.

"Watch where you're going, little bug!" Roz laughed.

"But you ran into *me*, Roz!" I slowly pushed myself to my feet.

Roz laughed harder.

Claudia glared at her. "You're not allowed to have a skateboard on the playground!"

Roz glared back.

"It's against the rules!" Claudia said.

"Not if I'm bringing it for show-and-tell!" Roz picked up her skateboard and grinned. "It's super special, isn't it?"

It was. But I wasn't going to tell Roz that. "It's okay," I said.

"Ha!" Roz said. "It's better than anything you have!"

"Ha!" I said. I pulled the baseball card from my pocket.

Roz grabbed it from my hand and looked at it. "Clyde Spinner?" she said.

"He was a pitcher who could throw a great curveball," I told her.

Roz grinned. "Like this?" She swung her arm back. She threw the card.

I watched it soar high into the air. It spun. It curved.

My baseball card flew toward the woods next to the playground.

Then it disappeared into the thick bushes.

chapter 3
Show-and-Tell

"My card!" I yelled.

Roz laughed as I ran toward the woods at the edge of the school playground.

I needed to hurry!

I needed to find my favorite baseball card before —

RING!

"Oh, no!" I said. "That's the bell."

I heard kids on the playground rush toward the school building.

"Hurry, Clyde!" Claudia yelled.

"I'm looking as fast as I can," I said. "But I don't see my baseball card."

"I mean, hurry and get in the building!" My sister pointed. Then she ran.

I turned and saw Principal Murphy walking toward me.

Kids are not allowed to leave the playground. Like I had.

So I ran.

Before Principal Murphy could yell at me, I was up the steps and in the school building.

I raced down the hallway. I slid around a corner. I dashed into my classroom.

"Looks like you're excited to be here, Clyde," Miss Plum, my teacher, said.

I nodded.

But I wasn't.

Well, I was glad to be away from Principal Murphy. But as I sat at my desk, all I could think about was my lost Clyde Spinner card.

"Got anything for show-and-tell, little bug?" Roz laughed as she walked past my desk. "Or did it fly away?"

"I'll find something," I said. "Something super special."

During the day, I looked and looked. By late afternoon I still had nothing — except the banana from my lunch.

"Show-and-tell time," Miss Plum said.

Kody showed the class a small dinosaur bone.

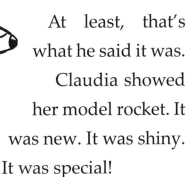

At least, that's what he said it was.

Claudia showed her model rocket. It was new. It was shiny. It was special!

Roz showed us her skateboard. It was super special. She tried to ride it. But Miss Plum told her, "Not in the classroom!"

Roz picked up her skateboard and grinned at me as she walked to her desk.

"Your turn, Clyde," Miss Plum said.

I gulped. I didn't know what to do. I had nothing for show-and-tell.

But then I got a super idea.

"Clyde?" Miss Plum said.

"I'll be right back," I said to my teacher.

I ran out of the classroom.

Claudia followed me into the hallway. "Miss Plum sent me to make sure you come back."

"I will." I grinned and bounced.

"You're getting too excited!" Claudia said.

"I know." I closed my eyes and thought about exciting things. Like banana pudding. Like turning into a monkey.

Like bringing a monkey to show-and-tell!

A wave of energy splashed through me.

My head started spinning. My heart raced.
Faster. And faster.

I sneezed.

chapter 4
Skateboard Monkey

CLYDE! STOP!

PRINCIPAL MURPHY MIGHT SEE YOU.

SHE'LL TOSS YOU OUT OF SCHOOL WHEN SHE CATCHES YOU!

YOU MEAN, _IF_ SHE CATCHES ME.

BOYS

I ALWAYS WEAR SHORTS UNDER MY PANTS. JUST IN CASE.

TA-DAH!

NOW, IT'S BACK TO CLASS.

AND THIS TIME NOBODY'S GOING TO LAUGH AT ME DURING SHOW-AND-TELL.

DON'T COUNT ON IT.

FORGET IT, CLYDE! I'M NOT GETTING IN TROUBLE, TOO.

ME? GET IN TROUBLE? HA!

LOOK! EVERYONE'S EXCITED TO SEE ME!

A MONKEY?

HE LOOKS FUNNY.

HE LOOKS HUNGRY.

HE LOOKS LIKE A BUG WHO NEEDS TO BE SQUASHED!

chapter 5
New Neighbors

Principal Murphy took me to the school office.

She took away Roz's skateboard.

Then she punished me for being out of my classroom by making me do something super tough.

She made me sit still.

Sometimes Principal Murphy keeps me after school. But when the final bell rang, she said, "Today, Clyde, I have something else I need to do."

So did I. I walked quickly out of the school building. Then I ran.

Claudia ran after me. "Are you okay?"

"I am now," I said. "I'm away from school and from Principal Murphy!"

"She's just doing her job." Claudia ran beside me. "She's trying to keep school free of troublemakers. And of monkeys."

"Ha!" I said. But I knew my sister was right. Like usual.

We ran around a corner and onto our block. We were almost home.

"Look, Clyde!" Claudia pointed to the house next to ours.

We slowed to a stop.

The big moving truck was gone.

"You think our neighbors have moved in?" Claudia asked.

There were no cars in the driveway. But I saw something white inside the window move as we walked toward the front door.

"Claudia! Clyde!"

It was Mom calling us from our house.

"Rats!" I said.

"We better go, Clyde," Claudia said.

Our parents had a rule. After school Claudia and I were to do our homework first. Then we could play.

"We'll come back later, Clyde." Claudia pulled me to our house.

I walked upstairs to my bedroom. I opened my math book.

Looking at homework problems made me sleepy. So I looked out my window at the house next to mine.

I wondered if my new neighbors had a kid my age. Someone who played soccer, like me. Or liked monkeys.

Like me.

I opened my window and grinned.

A wave of energy splashed through me.

My head started spinning. My heart raced. Faster. And faster.

I sneezed.

chapter 6
The Sneak

TA-DAH!

IT'S TIME TO STUDY...

...MY NEW NEIGHBORS!

I NEED TO BE CAREFUL.

AND QUIET.

AND SNEAKY.

HA! NO ONE WILL EVEN KNOW I'M HERE.

THERE'S NOTHING SNEAKIER THAN A MONKEY.

MEOW!

THIS IS BETTER THAN I EXPECTED.

I HOPE MY HUMAN NEIGHBORS ARE AS NICE AS YOU.

KNOCK! KNOCK!

HERE COMES ONE NOW.

WHO'S THERE?

chapter 7
Time to Move!

I was human! Again!

I quickly looked out my bedroom window.

Yikes!

My nightmare was real! Principal Murphy's car was in the driveway of the house next to mine.

She was my new neighbor!

I heard a knock on my bedroom door.

"I'll be right there," I said. I quickly dressed.

"Clyde?" It was Claudia's voice.

I opened the door.

"Didn't you hear Mom calling us?" my sister asked.

"No," I said.

Claudia looked at my face. "Are you okay, Clyde?"

"Yes. I mean, no. I mean . . . we have to move!" I yelled. "Principal Murphy is our new neighbor!"

Claudia and I looked out my window.

"I thought she lived at school," I said. "Or in a cave."

My sister chuckled.

We saw the principal's car. But not Principal Murphy.

"Why did she have to move into our neighborhood?" I asked.

"Our neighborhood is a nice place to live," Claudia said.

"You mean, it *was* a nice place to live," I said.

"Having Principal Murphy as a neighbor might not be so bad." Claudia tugged on my arm. "Come on, Clyde!"

I followed my sister down the steps.

But I couldn't stop worrying.

Having Principal Murphy as a neighbor was going to be horrible!

It was all I could think about — until I smelled the freshly baked cookies!

YUM!

I raced into the kitchen.

Being a monkey had made me hungry.

"I thought you two might need a break from doing homework," Mom said.

"We do!" I leaned toward the plate of chocolate chip cookies on the table.

"Good!" Mom said.

I reached for a cookie.

Mom pushed my hand away. "Because I'd like you to take these cookies to our new neighbor."

chapter 8
Principal Murphy

Claudia carried the plate of cookies out the door.

I tried to grab one. But my sister slapped my hand.

SLAP !

"Mom said these are for our new neighbor, Principal Murphy!" she said.

"We don't have to see the principal, do we?" I asked.

"Of course we do," Claudia said. "We can't just leave the cookies on her front step, ring the doorbell, and run."

"Why not?" I asked.

Claudia rolled her eyes.

"Come on, Clyde!" She stepped onto Principal Murphy's front porch and rang the doorbell.

The door swung open. Principal Murphy stood in the doorway. She stared down at us.

I gulped.

Claudia handed our principal the plate of cookies. "Welcome to the neighborhood!"

I waited for our principal to growl.

Instead, she smiled.

"Thank you, Claudia and Clyde," she said. "Would you like to come in?"

"No," I quickly said. "We need to get back to doing our homework."

Claudia gave me a surprised look.

Principal Murphy pointed to the cookies. "I could use some help eating these."

My stomach growled.

"Well, maybe we could come in," I said. "But only for a few cookies . . . I mean, only for a few minutes."

Principal Murphy led us inside.

I thought I would see wooden chairs and a big desk. Like in her office at school.

But the living room had two soft chairs. And a sofa. And a TV.

The principal set the cookies on a small table. "Help yourself," she said.

I grabbed and ate a few as I looked around. Boxes were everywhere. Some were open.

In one I spotted something I didn't expect. I raced toward the box.

"Baseball cards!" I shouted.

Principal Murphy smiled. "I've collected them since I was your age, Clyde." She showed me a signed Ty Homer card.

"That's worth a lot of money," I said. I looked through the box of cards. "These are amazing!"

Principal Murphy smiled.

Then I spotted a white cat poking her head into the room.

"Come, Muffin," Principal Murphy said. "These are our new neighbors."

The cat looked at Claudia and me. Then she raced out of the room.

"Muffin is a bit shy," Principal Murphy said. "But you'll meet her someday soon."

"I've already met her," I said.

"You have? When?" The principal looked surprised.

Claudia looked worried.

"I mean," I quickly said, "I can't wait to meet her."

"But right now, Clyde and I need to get back to our homework," Claudia said.

"Already?" I asked.

Claudia nodded.

I grabbed the last cookie and followed Principal Murphy to the front door.

"Thank you again, children. You're welcome to come back anytime." Principal Murphy smiled as Claudia and I left.

"So, what do you think of our new neighbor, Clyde?" Claudia asked as we walked home.

"I can't believe it!" I said.

"That Principal Murphy collects baseball cards?" Claudia asked.

"That Principal Murphy seems normal," I said. "And nice."

chapter 9
Trapped!

The next morning I jumped out of bed. I still couldn't believe it.

"Principal Murphy is nice," I said to Claudia as we raced to school.

But when I ran onto the playground, I saw Principal Murphy carrying her big net.

"A troublemaker is not going to run loose in my school!" the principal said. Then she waved her net in the air and continued searching for the monkey.

The monkey me.

"It's her job," Claudia said. "She's both a nice woman . . . and the school principal!"

I scratched my head. Then —

Suddenly, I was on the ground looking up at Roz.

"It's your fault Principal Murphy took my skateboard yesterday!" she yelled.

I didn't know what to say. So I ran.

I ran around the playground. When the bell rang, I ran inside to my classroom where I was safe from Roz. But not from Miss Plum.

My teacher wasn't happy when she found out I didn't have anything for show-and-tell. "Didn't you hear me tell the class yesterday we would finish show-and-tell today?" she asked.

"No," I said. "Because I was in the office."

Miss Plum wasn't happy about that, either.

"Please bring something to show-and-tell tomorrow, Clyde," she said.

"I will," I said.

When school was over I ran home and looked for something for show-and-tell.

I looked in my bedroom and in the basement. I looked outside and found . . . "Roz!"

She was standing on my front lawn. "We have some unfinished business, little bug!"

Standing next to her was Chopper, her bulldog. He grunted. He growled.

I ran.

I felt the ground behind me shake.

I am faster than Roz.

But not faster than Chopper.

I looked for a tree to climb.

There were none.

I looked at the large thornbush in front of me and quickly stopped.

And turned.

"You're trapped, little bug!" Roz said.

chapter 10
Good-bye, Little Bug!

My knees shook.

Roz looked angry.

Chopper looked hungry.

"What are you going to do?" I asked. "Squash me? Eat me?"

"No." Roz grinned. "We're going to do something even worse!"

Roz grabbed my arms. She pushed me to Principal Murphy's house.

The principal's car was not in the driveway. But there was a small truck parked in front of the house.

Roz pushed me to the tall fence around the principal's backyard. She opened the fence door and shoved me inside.

"Good-bye, little bug!" Roz said as though she would never see me again. Then she slammed the fence door shut and laughed.

Roz thought I was in trouble. Of course, I didn't tell Roz Principal Murphy wasn't home. Or that we were friends. But I did pretend to be scared. "Help! Help!" I yelled. "Let me out!"

I heard Chopper's happy bark. I heard Roz laugh louder. Then I heard them walk away from the fence.

"Ha! It worked!" I said to myself. Fooling Roz was fun.

I smiled and looked around. The back door to Principal Murphy's house was open.

I heard a bumping noise. I peeked in the doorway. I heard a cat's meow. Muffin sounded scared. So I stepped inside and walked to the front room.

A man was carrying the principal's box of baseball cards toward the front door. "I'm a mover, kid," he said when he saw me. "So stay out of my way!"

I walked back outside. But something didn't seem right.

"Wait a minute!" I said. "He's moving things out — not in!" I raced to the front of the house. I saw the man stepping into the small truck.

A woman was sitting on the front seat.

She was holding something white and fluffy.

"Muffin?" I said.

Muffin looked at me through the window. She was scared. And trapped!

"Stop!" I yelled. But the truck started moving. I had to do something. Fast!

"It's monkey time!" I said. I quickly jumped behind a bush.

I closed my eyes and thought of exciting things. Like eating cookies. Like tricking Roz. Like saving Muffin.

A wave of energy splashed through me.

My head started spinning. My heart raced. Faster. And faster.

I sneezed. "A-CHOO!"

chapter **11**
Cat Burglars

CATCH THAT MONKEY!

chapter 12
Help!

Claudia rode her bike toward me. "What's going on, Clyde?"

"I need help!" I said.

"But first, you need to put your clothes on." Claudia pulled them from her bike pack and handed them to me.

I quickly dressed. Then I ran.

"I need to catch the burglars," I said.

Claudia rode her bike behind me. "Aren't you running the wrong way, Clyde?"

"No. Because I need help. BIG help!" I said.

"Like the police?" Claudia asked.

"Yes," I said. "But the burglars might be gone before the police get there."

We hurried around a corner and onto the street where we lived.

"I need help from someone who's fast and not afraid of anything," I said. "Like Principal Murphy." I ran toward her house.

"What will you tell her?" Claudia asked.

"Nothing," I said. "There's no time to explain things to her."

I closed my eyes and thought about super exciting things.

Like flying a kite. Like climbing monkey bars. Like catching burglars with Principal Murphy's help!

A wave of energy splashed through me.

My head started spinning. My heart raced. Faster. And faster.

I sneezed. "A-CHOO!"

TA-DAH!

WHAT ARE YOU DOING, CLYDE?

I'M GOING IN TO GET PRINCIPAL MURPHY.

SHE ISN'T GOING TO BE HAPPY TO SEE YOU.

THAT'S MY PLAN.

THANKS, CLAUDIA! NOW I NEED TO GO...

... IN THE DOOR THIS TIME.

BACK INSIDE...

I CAN'T WAIT FOR HELP!

THE BURGLARS MIGHT GET AWAY.

IT'S MONKEY TIME!

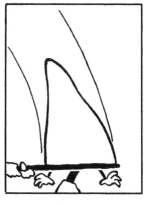

THE POLICE ARE HERE!

GOOD WORK, PRINCIPAL MURPHY!

I HAVE MUFFIN AND MY BASEBALL CARDS BACK!

I DID IT!

WE DID IT!

chapter **14**
Monkey Me—Again!

"Slow down, Clyde!" Claudia yelled the next morning.

I grabbed a banana off the breakfast table. "I can't wait for show-and-tell," I said.

"What are you bringing?" Claudia asked.

"Principal Murphy." I ate the banana as I ran out the front doorway.

Claudia raced after me and grabbed my arm. "You're bringing our principal?"

I nodded.

"I went to her house yesterday after she helped catch the burglars," I said.

"Why, Clyde?" Claudia asked.

"Principal Murphy has baseball cards that are super special!" I said.

"And worth lots of money," Claudia said.

"So I asked if I could bring some of her cards to school for show-and-tell," I said.

"And she let you?" Claudia asked.

"Sort of," I said. "Principal Murphy told me she'd feel safer if she showed the cards to the class herself."

I ran onto the playground. "So I'm bringing Principal Murphy to show-and-tell. And she's bringing her baseball cards."

"Super!" Claudia said.

"Super special!" I said.

"And look at this!" I pulled a baseball card from my pocket. I showed it to Claudia.

"A Clyde Spinner card?" Claudia said.

I grinned. "Principal Murphy had two. So she gave it to me to replace the one I lost in the playground bushes."

Claudia smiled at me. "I told you Principal Murphy would be a nice neighbor."

"I think she even likes me," I said.

"But not the monkey you," Claudia said. "At least, not in school."

I thought about Principal Murphy and her large net.

"So you better be careful!" Claudia said.

When the bell rang, I raced into school. I ran down the hallway. I dashed into my classroom.

It was hard to wait. But finally in the afternoon, Miss Plum told the class, "It's time for show-and-tell."

She looked at me. "So, what did you bring to show us, Clyde?"

I heard Roz chuckle.

"I'll be right back, Miss Plum," I said.

"I better go with you," Claudia said. She followed me into the hallway.

I hurried toward the office.

"Be careful, Clyde!" Claudia said.

"Why?" I bounced as I got closer.

"You're getting too excited!" Claudia said. She tried to grab my arm, but missed.

A wave of energy splashed through me.

My head started spinning. My heart raced. Faster. And faster.

I sneezed. "A-CHOO!"

Timothy Roland

likes monkeys, eating bananas, and finding funny story ideas. He finds ideas by remembering, by thinking, and by looking around.

Timothy lives and works in Pennsylvania. None of his neighbors own a pet monkey. If they did, Timothy could watch the monkey to get ideas for writing and drawing pictures for his Monkey Me books. But first, he would need to hide his bananas.

Monkey Me

QUESTIONS & ACTIVITES

CAN YOU ANSWER THESE QUESTIONS ABOUT MONKEY ME AND THE NEW NEIGHBOR?

At first, how do Clyde and Claudia feel about Principal Murphy moving in next door?

What does Clyde have in common with Principal Murphy?

How does Clyde get Principal Murphy to the burglars' house without talking?

How does Principal Murphy feel about the monkey at the end of the book?

Write a comic strip about Muffin and Clyde! Make sure to explain what makes them such good friends.